I0456275

AFTERLIFE CODE

by J. M. Erickson

Afterlife Code

All rights reserved
Copyright 2018 J. M. Erickson
www.jmericksonindiewriter.com

Editors: Suzanne M. Owen and Kirkus Editorial

Cover design: Cathy Helms, Avalon Graphics, LLC
www.avalongraphics.org

Layout and eBook conversion: eB Format
www.ebformat.com

Publisher: J. M. Erickson
www.jmericksonindiewriter.net

ISBN (MOBI Format): 978-1-942708-48-3
ISBN (ePub Format): 978-1-942708-49-0
ISBN (Softcover): 978-1-942708-50-6

No part of this book may be reproduced in any form or by any electronic or mechanical means, including information storage and retrieval systems, without permission in writing by the author, except in the case of brief quotations embodied in critical articles and reviews.

This is a work of pure fiction. Although some places in this book exist, any resemblance to real people, living or dead, or events is purely coincidental.

Printed in the United States of America

Other Works by J. M. Erickson

Action/Adventure Thrillers

Albatross: Birds of Flight—Book One
Raven: Birds of Flight—Book Two
Eagle: Birds of Flight—Book Three
Falcon: Birds of Flight—Book Four
Flight of the Black Swan

Action/Adventure Science Fiction

Future Prometheus I: Emergence & Evolution—Novellas I & II
Future Prometheus II: Revolution, Successions, & Resurrections—
Novellas III, IV & V Intelligent Design: Revelations
Intelligent Design: Apocalypse
The Prince: Lucifer's Origins
Future Prometheus: The Series
Intelligent Design: Revelations to Apocalypse
Time Is for Dragonflies and Angels

CHAPTER ONE

"Just think about it. I know your work is very important, but there's more to life."

"Mother, I'm thirty-seven years old, and the chances of me having children have dwindled to nothing. Why do you keep talking about this?" Dr. Melanie Sage asked. It was still morning, and she had already been up nearly all night. Her pajamas, the ones she wore during the workweek from Monday to Wednesday, still felt warm from her bed. Her bedroom looked similar to her work space, with more computers, tablets, and other computing gear. She paused to think about the level of radiation she might be getting from all the electronics that surrounded her at night but then dispelled that thought as soon as she picked up her smartphone. She regretted not checking caller identification.

"I saw Gary yesterday at the library, and he was asking about you. He's been divorced for years, and every time I see him, he asks how you're doing."

For a moment, Sage wondered why her mother sounded muffled. A cold?

"Maybe you should download your books and movies and stop going to the library."

There was a brief silence on the phone. A vague memory of a tall, dark-skinned, dark-eyed man fluttered in front of her, but she lost the image. Remembering faces had never been her strong point.

"When are you coming home? Your father and I haven't seen you in eight months," her mother said. Sage decided not to answer the question and switched topics instead.

"I have isolated the majority of the code and now need more computer input and simulations to see if I can simply create a radio frequency to transmit to my implant."

"To transmit what? You shouldn't be messing with your implant. That's a medical procedure, and I don't want you to mess with your emotions," her mother warned.

By now, Sage had her feet comfortably in her bed/bathroom slippers and was en route to brush her teeth with her sonar brush, then do a facial scrub and fifteen-minute cleansing procedure that was so engrained she could do it in her sleep. And there had been three times she did just that.

"Mother, I'm not doing any kind of surgery. I am simply transmitting a simple code that could enhance the part of my brain that helps with recognizing and engaging the neural structures to enhance their functioning." Sage struggled to keep the language simple. While her mother and father were bright, they were social workers and teachers, not computer science students.

"I just think that you should not be messing with things you don't know about."

Sage found herself taken aback. She was in front of her mirror and refocused her gaze from the matted hair and oily skin to her expression. She could identify "surprise," and it was fortuitous that she was able to feel the emotion and see the corresponding reaction in the mirror.

"Mother, this is coding, computer science, and radio frequencies. With two doctorates in computer science and mathematics, I think I can field this. I'll call you on Friday at the usual time. I'm working late, so I may not answer if I'm onto something."

There was a brief silence until her mother spoke again.

"All right, dear. Dad and I love you."

"I love you too," Sage said. While the words came out, she was not feeling that emotion. Still, it was common-courtesy child–parent communication to terminate in this fashion, as it reduced hostility for future conversations.

Rather than waiting to hear the phone close out, Sage clicked off first. She was feeling behind in getting ready, and she wanted to start her morning waking rituals.

"Why does she do that?" she said.

There was no one in her apartment. She liked it that way so when she would talk to herself she never had to worry about others either hearing or criticizing. She shifted focus back on what she was doing.

"I got to get going."

CHAPTER TWO

"What are you doing here?" The young man was wide awake, but his face looked oily, and his hair was not combed, as if he had just woken up from a deep slumber. He was also in his underwear and T-shirt even though it was ten o'clock in the morning. In contrast stood his father, a perfectly groomed middle-aged man wearing a vintage-style three-piece suit, looking at his son with some disbelief but long-established acceptance.

"Let me guess. You and your sister are working from home again?" Robert Cobb said. He already knew the answer. Even though the elevator was out and he'd had to climb four flights of stairs, Cobb was not as winded as he thought he would be; the consistent choice of wearing a three-piece suit was to help cover his stomach and expanded backside. He'd been reveling in that thought when his son had abruptly opened the door.

"I thought you were the pizza guy. We ordered stuff an hour ago," said.

"What? It's ten in the morning. Who orders pizza in the morning?" Cobb asked.

Once inside, Cobb took in his son and daughter's massive apartment, with its huge windows nearly boarded up to keep all natural light at bay and five visible workstations in the middle of the nearly empty living area where you would have expected expensive furnishing and entertainment centers. Instead, there were old-fashioned beanbags, sleeping bags, and the five computer stations, each holding double layers of four large monitors and networked CPUs of varying sizes with corresponding power strips taped down on an otherwise elegant hardwood floor. What struck Cobb the most was the unnatural electronic-blue lighting emanating from the three active stations. Just to add to the surreal scene, three people close to his son's age, in varying degrees of dress, lounged in the vast, dark apartment. They seemed to keep warm from the heat generated by the CPUs. Another parent might have been shocked or at the very least surprised. Cobb was far from it.

"We've been gaming all night, and we figured out how South Korea and the rest of Asia have been able to beat our system. We're close to predicting their defensive and deployment strategies," his son explained.

The military vernacular and extensive computer network were only missing seasoned soldiers or spies. Instead, there was his son and his friends, still in their pajamas and sleeping gear.

"Hi, Mr. Cobb," one of the gamers said. Another looked over and gave him a thumbs-up sign. Cobb waved to them both, and they went right back into their gaming. He had known both of them as children in the neighborhood—they'd grown up with his two children, James and Jennifer. They had always played computer games together. If Cobb had not witnessed his son and daughter winning $7 million in a *fourth*-prize professional championship gaming event, he would have long since pushed his children to get "real" jobs and "real" professions and "real" lives. Although he had not been in their lives when they were younger because of psychiatric issues and injuries, he was sure he would have said the age-old parental motto, "You think you can make a living playing games?" Three years ago, when they put together their team and won a world video-gaming championship, he had been shocked. Their mother was always supportive of them, and it paid off.

"Where's your sister?" Cobb asked.

"I'm going to get her up in twenty minutes. I needed her to sleep so that she can have fresh eyes on console five. I was just going to get things ready and the pizza before we start. Anything wrong?"

"No, I just had called last night and texted you both this morning and was making sure you both weren't dead." Cobb suddenly had a thought: his daughter was notorious for taking forever to get ready in the morning.

"Wait a minute—Jen will get up and get right to playing without spending life and a day fixing her hair and prepping herself?"

His son clearly saw where he was going with this.

"A multimillion-dollar prize will do that, Dad."

"That can help a lot of things."

His son stopped combing his hair with his hand and gave him a lopsided smile.

"You know this is our busy season, Dad."

Cobb had genuinely forgotten that they were in the middle of a major tournament. "Actually, I'm embarrassed to say I forgot. Now that I know you're both alive, I'll head to work."

"Wait, you really came here to make sure that we were all right? You're worse than Mom," James said.

"Well . . . I guess I worry for no reason."

"Why don't you stay?" his son said. Although the words were right, the tone behind them was weak. Having been young once, Cobb easily could tell that James was itching to eat and get back to his gaming. Even as he asked, he pushed a button on an old-style desktop CPU, and his eight monitors erupted to life, with fans and power whirring from below the metal-and-glass desk.

"No, I got a client in thirty minutes, and I was just checking on you and Jen. Just give me a text when you're done—we can celebrate. And say hello to your mother and her guy-friend."

"You know she and her 'guy-friend' have been together for five years. His name is Jack," James said.

"Hmm," was all Cobb said. He headed back to the door. His son came up from behind to say good-bye. Before opening the door, Cobb gave him a hug. He could feel his rib cage.

"Could you eat something, please? And maybe you and your sister go out to see the sun and breathe in actual air?" Cobb asked.

"Sure can—in two weeks, after we win the top prize."

"How much money this time?"

"Seventeen million."

Cobb found himself trying to get his head around the massive number. Growing up poor made it hard. And the fact that his daughter and son were millionaires and entrepreneurs was something that was hard to grasp.

"It's a great country," Cobb said out of astonishment of how one could get rich in America. Cobb opened the door, and a tall, tired-looking, middle-aged man was holding five pizza boxes and bags of presumably plates and liters of liquids. James pushed his father aside to get the food. Cobb moved out of the way as quickly as he could and headed to the stairs.

"Hey, Mr. Cobb," the pizza delivery man said, "that orange door downstairs is much better. Makes it wicked easier for the new guys to find." Cobb took a moment to figure out that he was not being addressed; his son was. *Hmm . . . my son is Mr. Cobb too . . .*

"Much better than the street number and GPS," James said.

"Yup, you can see the door is different from all the other black doors, to start."

Cobb watched his son and the delivery man for a few seconds more and started his walk to work. It was blocks away, but it would be a nice walk.

"Love you, Dad," his son said.

"Love you both," he said.

Although he was clearly proud of his two young adult children and all they had achieved, somehow, living on pizza and soda and playing computer games in a dark apartment in a multimillion-dollar complex with a pool, gym, and all amenities seemed odd to him.

CHAPTER THREE

"Dr. Karlsson is pissed. I've been able to get you more time in the 3-D virtual computer server, but she's already looking into cutting back more hours and energy."

Sage really liked her assistant, Paula Dirac; she was very intelligent, a savant with numbers, and really good at sensing when things were going to go south and getting her out of trouble. After four years of working together, they had established a way of communicating in a sea of people and monitors without appearing as if they were talking. Dirac would be peering at a set of tablets near Sage's workstation, and Sage would go on as if she were working. And while she was indeed working, two of her monitors were displaying a series of moving symbols, numbers, and formulae that was difficult but not impossible to follow. She adjusted her smartphone and continued to download and translate the data into yet another algorithm to upload later.

"I'm finishing it up now, Paula. Thank you," Sage said. She felt gratitude for her assistant's kindness and her keeping Sage out of trouble.

"No problem. Dr. Karlsson is fighting with the Department of Defense about who really runs the program, and the less we engage it, even remotely, the better. By the way, how is it going? You really think you can improve upon a code that will enhance your implant? I know it's not surgery, and I'm guessing you already have a reset button or program ready, but how will you know if it goes in the shitter?" Unlike her mother's earlier concern, Sage thoroughly understood Dirac's point.

"Twofold solution: I do have a reset, and you have my password for my files. If anyone can figure it out, you can," Sage said. She smiled at the thought of being so close to a code that could help her autism. She was doing well, but to be able to focus on important things rather than social things was entirely exciting. Her excitement led to another thought.

"So how is your field of study going, Paula?"

Sage always felt interested in her assistant's work. Paula was not only her assistant as well as the assistant for a team of twelve others, but she was also in her final years as a doctoral student. There was even talk that she was a distant relation to Paul Dirac, the theoretical physicist that unified quantum mechanics and relativity theory into one equation. What was evident was that she was smart, and she had a way of making Sage feel . . . good? It was definitely a positive feeling: Paula always made her feel welcomed and comfortable. And in those rare moments when Paula was out, she was not able to work and felt compelled to bring her food. Her mother said she must love her, but it felt deeper than that.

"You'd think that finding a new expression for matter–antimatter would be easier," Dirac said with a smile. By now, Sage could tell when she was being sarcastic.

"If anyone gets it, it will be you."

"Yes," Dirac said and then added, "all right, Dr. Sage, Dr. Karlsson is in the building, and she will be in her office in less than three minutes based on her gait. She's either pissed at the Department of Defense or she's excited about something; whatever you're going to do, finish it up."

Sage nodded and sensed Paula moving off.

"Thank you," Sage said. She was not sure Dirac heard her, but she kept the program running. She stopped it after sixty seconds at a place where she could pick up. She knew there was something missing, but she had learned to trust her assistant and moved to clear out of the 3-D computer server before Dr. Karlsson found her.

It took another minute for her monitors to shift to another project she was working on. Once it was up and running, she stretched her back and then stood up. Looking over several dozen scientists and technicians, she saw Paula Dirac looking at her and smiling. Sage gave her a nod to let her know she was out. She was hit with the thought that Dirac could have nodded, but she smiled instead. She wondered if that was a social cue for something.

"I really hope I can get this code to work."

CHAPTER FOUR

"*Myaamia* **might sound like** *Miami*, but it's a First Nation name. And it's probably where the city got its name from. Why the curiosity?" Robert M. Cobb asked his young client.

"I've been wondering what the *M* on your diplomas stood for. You Native American?"

"Mostly black but a big part First Nation. You know, we've been working together for three years, and you've just now decided to ask me about my origins?"

The young man sat at ease for a marine. Even in his civilian clothes—silk floral shirt, khaki shorts, and sandals—his build, chiseled features, and short haircut screamed military. With sharp features of Arab descent, his eleven o'clock appointment was vigilant and ready for anything. In contrast, Robert Cobb was older, relaxed, and not too far from disheveled even though his out-of-date three-piece suit had just been dry-cleaned. He thought of his adult children making millions playing video games. *It's a great country.*

"I would have thought that you had DNA done on me when we met," Cobb said. He hoped his client took the jab well; back when they first started, his client was hostile, paranoid, nearly xenophobic, and certainly misanthropic.

"I might have given the impression I knew it all then, but I was pretty messed up. An IED will do that," the client said.

"It sure will," Cobb said. He was distracted for just a moment. He opened the color-coded, relatively thin file on his client and went to the first page. He read the first lines of the admission note and smiled to himself.

Nothing got by his client still. Even though he was profoundly better—he no longer needed sedatives during the day and could actually sit down and not react to stray sounds, no matter how minute, or movements, no matter how fast—his present relaxed state would be better called "hypervigilant" as opposed to "traumatic-brain-injured posttrauma victim with psychotic features."

"I'm just reading that three years ago, the Veterans Administration was not too hopeful about your situation. But between the therapy and bio-limbic device, you have really exceeded all expectations. Fortunately for you, I was here."

Cobb could barely keep from laughing at his own remark. His client chuckled, which would have been an unheard-of possibility two years ago, before the brain device was put in his head. Cobb was sure his young client's intercranial limbic device was state-of-the-art technology, with a stabilizing current to keep the shielding in place. This would not only keep posttrauma anxiety and depression from flooding his brain, but it would also keep stray radio waves out. His device was probably faster at balancing neurogenesis to process traumatic memories in ways that were no longer debilitating.

I wonder if I should get an upgrade. It's been twenty years. His hand instinctively rubbed the back of his skull. Finding the healed scar was not hard to do through his thinned hair. He refocused on where he was. He then wondered if he could reprogram it to help him lose weight too.

"Well, my young man, you're medically cleared to return to active duty. The technicians at the lab and the psychiatrists cleared you, and I've got nothing to keep you from going back to the service. Why you would want fieldwork is beyond me, but I suppose being a marine is a way of life that can't just be dropped, even if it almost killed you."

"*Almost* is the key word there, Bob. But you were in the marines, right?"

Cobb nearly fell out of his seat.

"No . . . not at all. I was a US Army Ranger thirty-two years ago, but my first mission put an end to a short, lackluster career," Cobb said. He noted it was said with a lack of emotion. It had been that way for more than three decades. He looked at his client, who gave him a look that obviously meant he wanted to hear more. Cobb was hesitant. He wasn't sure how telling his client was helpful to him. He flashed to his young adult children and was happy they never had to serve, not that he served very long.

"Aren't you the one who says understanding events is the best way to heal? You know, 'Trauma is the brain's natural response to unnatural situations. Telling the story, the narrative, helps,'" his client said.

"Impressive. And here I thought you were sleeping when I went on," Cobb said. He was impressed. He did believe that trauma had to be talked out, but it was the biotechnological brain implant that really made it all work.

"Well?" his young client prodded. Dissuading him was far from probable now. Cobb took mere seconds to pull the story up as he remembered.

"In short, I was part of a search and rescue team in the Middle East, and the guy in front of me stepped on an IED and died. I was lucky to be hit mostly by him, and then my head hit a wall. The wall didn't move, so my skull accommodated. I was the one in need of rescuing. Head trauma and the events messed me up for years. Nothing worked for me, and I was discharged from active duty and then from the service entirely. The drinking kept a lot of the voices down and helped with sleep, but it nuked my marriage and made getting my duties completed and eventually holding on to a job not possible. If it wasn't for biotechnology and what the Navy research guys and gals came up with for brain implanting and sorting out the biochemistry of the limbic system, I probably wouldn't be here."

"Weren't those early models . . . ah . . . flawed?"

"They sure were," Cobb said. "Periodically, a stray radio-frequency wave can excite my implant. It causes some fading or graying out, like getting up too fast from sitting. That's what it's like for me. Others get seizures and stuff. I'm lucky with the mild side effects."

"So it was just the technology that helped? What about the narrative thing?"

"That was part two for me. The talking therapy, the cognitive-behavioral therapy, really helped me make sense of everything. The biotechnology calmed my mind, and the therapy helped rewire it into a coherent self. My therapist at the time, Dr. Gerson, always said, 'It's always about the story. People need the story to make sense of the world; no matter how good, bad, or evil, it's always about the story, the narrative.'"

Cobb fell quiet for a moment. Images of meeting with his own therapist stayed with him. Even though he had died so many years ago, Cobb still remembered him as if it were just yesterday. By the time they had met, he was in his sixties; he was tall, with a hefty stomach and piercing brown eyes. The eyes were always moving, as if he were looking for the answers to all his psychiatric questions.

"He's the big reason why I went back to school and became a therapist. I like to think I'm doing his work now."

"Sounds like he was a character."

"He was, especially back when he was younger, I guess. He would recite this old Latin proverb: 'Live your own life, for you will die your own death.' He did both well."

Cobb watched his client nod as if he understood. Cobb got up from his chair, which faced the client, and moved to his desk, where an official document awaited his signature. If signed, it meant his client could return to active service if he wanted to.

"With respect, Bob, how come you look in such . . . ah . . . in such good shape? I mean no disrespect, but you've been discharged for more than two decades. And while the suits might hide stuff, it doesn't take much to figure out you're in good shape."

"So this must be our last session for a while, all the questions."

"Just curious, Bob."

Cobb smiled, happy that his client was in such a place where he could be genuinely interested in others.

"I like to think that forty-five is the new thirty. I'm also lucky that my genetics are responsive to weight lifting, high volume, low weight. I still have my stomach, though." Cobb's hand fell on his slightly bulging vest.

"Hmm. Well, it's working."

"Thanks."

Checking his watch, he could see the hour was nearly up. He sensed his client was behind him, so he finished reading the letter and made sure to sign and date it. When he turned, his client was patiently waiting.

"I know you young people lift heavy, but those days are gone for me," Cobb added as he handed him the document. The young man looked briefly at it to make sure it was all signed and dated. Once done, he stuck his right hand out to shake. Cobb grabbed it and gave a firm handshake. It was not too different from the other times he had ended his sessions with him, but today was a big day.

"I'll see you in about three months for a checkup. It's been great working with you," Cobb said. For a moment, he could swear his eyes were welling just a bit. His client took notice.

"The benefits of getting older—expression of emotion is permissible even if you are an old veteran," Cobb said.

"It's been great working with you. Thank you." His client's voice sounded as if it was cracking just a bit, as if he was choked up. As expected, his client nodded briefly, aware that he did not want to demonstrate any sadness, retreated to the office door, opened it, and stepped out without closing it.

"Take care," Cobb said to an empty room. His voice was well absorbed by the upholstered furniture and the heavy rug and drapes. His well-appointed, relatively large office made him smile as he remembered his children's apartment. He moved to close his office door so that he could write a clinical note. Instead of writing, he found he needed a mental break. With just ten minutes between clients, he opened a file drawer and extracted eight four-inch aerodynamic throwing knives and put them on the corner of the desk. He knew he would have to put them in their carry pouch, but he kept them loose just so he could take a moment between clients to throw knives at his dart board. Their balance was perfect. He moved quickly and cleared the darts to make room for his knife throwing. He was glad he had long since reinforced the back of the dart board to accommodate the force each knife would expend. He was hoping his grouping would be better.

He moved to the side of his desk, giving him the extra distance he wanted for his throws. His suit was restrictive, so he took off the jacket and rolled up his sleeves, which gave him the appearance of a busy executive or legal counsel rather than a clinical social worker about to throw knives.

Cobb put one foot in front of the other. It was both his old shooting stance and fighting stance, but now it was his knife-throwing stance. He locked his dominant eye on the target a few feet away. It appeared more as a blurred image as he focused on the tip of the throwing knife. Before hurling the light, sharp metal knife, he smiled.

"It's really not a bad life I've got going here."

CHAPTER FIVE

"You, Melanie, are pretty messed up to think of things like this. The code for the neocortex cranial device is not meant to be screwed around with. And just because your autism is stabilized and level doesn't mean you can screw around with the device's code," Dr. Agnes Karlsson said. She was standing over Sage's computer desk in a large, hermetically sealed auditorium with many more desks. The difference was that the sea of desks was dark, and the hall was empty except for the two women and three pairs of uniformed guards in the middle of the Biotechnology and Behavioral Science Department of the Naval Research Institute.

Paula Dirac had warned her that Dr. Karlsson had been in a bad mood the past couple of days. She really didn't expect that Dr. Karlsson would be able to figure out what she was doing, as she was sure the data was raw. *How could she know?*

Sage did her best to refocus on the present to make sure she picked up on all social cues so as to retreat as quickly as possible. Dr. Karlsson was a tall woman of Swedish descent and was dressed as if she was heading out for a formal occasion or, more likely, had just attended one. The elegant, midnight-blue, semi-glittering dress with formfitting waist made her look both sensual and imperious at the same time. While typically not her strength, Sage could see that the use of gold accessories made an impressive statement of class and distinction.

"I'm sorry, Dr. Karlsson. I had an idea and thought it would be best not to connect to the 3-D computer server from the outside, so I came in—"

"And you tripped three silent alarms and triggered a critical incident investigation with internal affairs, and now I'll have the brass up my ass," Dr. Karlsson interrupted. Sage saw her boss's expression continue to turn red, making her appearance contrast with her outfit. She did her best not only to focus but to keep her smartphone out of sight for fear that it would be taken. The guards were also looking annoyed, but it was confusing, as three of the six were hiding smiles. Reading facial expressions was new to her— she'd been attempting to do so for just five of her thirty-seven years of coping with autism. With the ability to read social cues better and not be hampered down by focusing on the relatively minor things in life, she had been able to become far more creative. Now she was really onto something big, something her cranial device was never coded to do: increase data processing at a faster rate not by requiring massive growth in neurons but, rather, by pruning back stray unused neural networks. She had successfully transferred the new code via radio-frequency wave to her smartphone to avoid detection mere seconds before the soldiers and her boss showed up.

"I don't think my autism is 'cured' as much as it's managed," Sage said. "I think I just got excited about creating a new method to streamline neural connections without the need for inciting neurogenesis," she explained.

Her boss's face remained a rose red, and her eyes narrowed. No autism could get in the way of interpreting that her boss was really angry and thinking of some punishment to fit the crime. In many ways, the fact that her boss was similar to her mother in expressiveness had made it possible for her to work in the department for more than ten years as a consultant. It was twenty seconds before her boss spoke.

"Dr. Sage, I want you to go home, think about how you might have handled this situation better and managed your zeal, and explain it to me at 0900 hours. After that, I want you to see Bob Cobb and see if you can work out another plan that allows you to be less impulsive and more focused on your job," Dr. Karlsson said.

"Yes, Dr. Karlsson. I'll do that."

As always, Sage was impressed with how her boss was fair even when angry. While expressive like her mother, she was just as fair even when she was angry with her.

"And get out of the building. You two—escort her out of my facility," Dr. Karlsson said to two guards whose grim expressions softened. They must have thought the situation was humorous. Sage was having a hard time figuring out why.

Sage stood up and pulled her light jacket over her pajamas and bed/bathroom slippers. She had the brilliant coding sequence when she awoke from a deep sleep and just needed to check it out. She had no idea what time it was.

She was self-conscious that she was poorly dressed for being at work.

"Really, Dr. Sage? You came here in the middle of the night in your PJs?" Dr. Karlsson said. Her tone and expression seemed to convey more of a question, so Sage nodded. Before she passed her boss, she did take notice of her attire as a means of practicing reciprocity. She remembered her mother's advice about always commenting on how nice someone looks when the person is clearly dressed for some important activity. And because Dr. Karlsson typically wore all-black clothes with her lab coat, it seemed appropriate to comment on her evening wear.

"By the way, Dr. Karlsson, you look very nice tonight," Sage said.

A guard behind her burst out laughing and swiftly recovered when a glare from Dr. Karlsson fell upon him. Sage looked about and saw the others trying to stifle their own laughter. She knew she had made a mistake and that talking to Mr. Cobb would be helpful in that regard, for sure. Right now, Sage was just hoping that she would be able to escape. She planned to keep her mouth shut.

"I'm sorry, Dr. Karlsson."

"Yes, well, who wants to see the entire *Phantom of the Opera*?" Dr. Karlsson said.

Sarcasm or not, Sage couldn't tell, and she didn't want to ask. She decided to keep her head low and walk out under escort before she said anything more.

Three minutes later, she found herself outside of the Naval Research Institute in the new Charlestown Navy Yard in Charlestown, Massachusetts. It was colder than she remembered. She took out her smartphone and first made sure she had the data on her RF app. Then she looked at the time.

"One thirty-four! What was I thinking?" she said to herself. She pulled her light jacket around her thin body, clad in very old superhero pajamas that were still functional despite the years. It was also Wednesday night, and it would be time to change to Thursday-to-Sunday pajamas. But now that she had worn them outside, the debate was short on keeping these specific pajamas as sleepwear for bed.

She thought about calling Paula Dirac but stopped herself. She wondered why she always wanted to call her when things went wrong, rather than her mother or father. *Hmm . . . maybe I do love her as a friend?*

CHAPTER SIX

Cobb sat farther back in his seat, his hand rubbing his temples, while at the same time trying to keep from laughing. As soon as he heard the voicemail from Dr. Karlsson, he knew that Dr. Melanie Sage would be in his office, repeating verbatim the discussion of the entire situation that had transpired. Although he wasn't completely surprised by his client's difficulty in capturing all the subtleties of nonverbal communication and reading social cues, he was impressed by how her brain implant made her far better at those skills and had helped her develop an enjoyable personality. When she got to how she had commented on her boss's formal evening dress just prior to finding she had been interrupted from a grand evening out, then talked about her pajamas and the need to get a new set, he just had to sit still and let it all sink in.

"Speaking of which, you look very nice today. I see you went with a charcoal-gray three-piece suit today. I notice you wear that one on Thursdays," Sage said.

"I am a little obsessive about what I wear, but I think it's more of a pattern, though. I don't plan it that way," he said.

"How is being obsessive and adhering to a pattern different?"

"*Obsessive* would imply an inability to deviate from a thought, which in turn leads to rigid, compulsive behaviors to ease stress. Having a pattern implies consistency, yet with the flexibility to adapt to an evolving situation, future planning, and a capacity to change course without the need to be rigid."

Cobb watched Sage process the distinction.

"Both yield behaviors that reduce tension and minimize anxiety, correct?"

It was Cobb's turn to think. He had to agree.

"Yes, that's accurate. I guess it's the state of urgency and the flexibility that are important distinctions. I never thought of it that way."

He was still pondering the difference while Sage went on with her line of thinking.

"I find it far easier to plan my wardrobe by day and function in addition to lunch. In fact, it was this increase in executive functioning that got me thinking about my implant."

Cobb felt the corners of his mouth curl up slightly. The woman's IQ was off the charts, but he was thrilled to see that her skills in small talk, observation, and flow of conversation and changing cognitive sets were all in solid use—skills she didn't have at all prior to the implant to manage her autism.

Even as the story unraveled, he noticed that Sage's expression was far more animated and bordered on a cheerful tone rather than her usual deadpan, serious presentation. Her appearance—white lab coat covering a tan blouse and her typical olive-green slacks and functional shoes—was out of step with her more colorful presentation that day.

His thoughts traveled to the morning light coming in through his blinds. It was a brilliant June day, and he knew he would have to stay ahead of the heat by keeping the sun out of his office. He thought about taking his jacket off but decided to keep it on. Typically, he would have to turn on the overhead fluorescent lights, but not this morning. Before he could move to close the blinds just a little more, his client's voice brought him back to the conversation. He knew he had missed some of what she'd said already.

"So after Dr. Karlsson reiterated the policies about after-hours access and the need to follow strict protocols going forward, she said she wanted me to meet with you first. As it turns out, this is quite fortuitous, as I was hoping you would be present while I try this brief experiment. Your clinical expertise and familiarity with my case will be valuable," Sage said.

Cobb sat a bit straighter as he watched her pull out her smartphone. She swiped through a couple of screens, finally found an app, and activated it as she spoke.

"By augmenting the code for the intercranial limbic-cortex implant, I should be able to leave the stabilizing code for the autism biometrics alone while enhancing efficiency without neurogenesis." As she continued to look down, he saw her smile for a second and push a button, presumably to open an application.

"More likely, it will take milliseconds to download," he heard her say. Although it was clear that she was still talking, his hearing seemed to fail, and his vision began to tunnel. And while he was sure he had never had a seizure before, he felt like his brain was "fizzy," and his limbs tingled.

No . . . what the hell . . . is that, ah . . . something with a radio frequency . . .

Before he completely grayed out, he thought he made out Sage's expression. It was that of concern. He saw her get up out of the chair and reach for him. Upon contact, he felt his brain and body erupt with a heat wave or some electrical surge that came alive as soon as she touched him. Before fading out completely, he felt a weight on him and still more heat. Suddenly, there was darkness and silence while the heat subsided. Robert M. Cobb felt light and calm.

~

Dr. Melanie Sage always found her chats with Mr. Cobb interesting. He had been there from the start to help her with reading emotions, expressions, and social cues, which allowed her to fit in with her work group. As the resident employee-assistant specialist assigned to her agency, she found him to be invaluable to her transition. Even after the brain implant, when her need for him greatly declined, she would periodically see him. Lately, it was typically due to some kind of infraction of work rules or policies. Ever since her implant was put in, removing her need to focus on day-to-day social tasks, she had really taken off with ideas. They all clashed with others' ideas, creating conflicts. Of late, Dr. Karlsson had taken to involving Mr. Cobb.

"She was not appreciative of my comment about her dress. I should have known that I must have interrupted something. She said I interrupted her from attending *Phantom of the Opera*, but she arrived well after one in the morning, so I am sure the opera was over. She did mention something this morning about how Dr. Walsh was fatigued, too, as if it was somehow connected."

A new thought launched to the foreground, and her hand shot to her pocket.

Oh, let me find the program and download it to my cranial interface. If it works, I can tell Mr. Cobb about it. If it doesn't, it's back to the drawing board . . .

"So after Dr. Karlsson reiterated the policies about after-hours access and the need to follow strict protocols going forward, she said she wanted me to meet with you first. As it turns out, this is quite fortuitous, as I was hoping you would be present while I try this brief experiment. Your clinical expertise and familiarity with my case will be valuable," Sage said.

That didn't take long. Hmm . . . I wonder if it will work now.

"By augmenting the code for the intercranial limbic-cortex implant, I should be able to leave the stabilizing code for the autism biometrics alone while enhancing efficiency without neurogenesis."

Finally, the application for the program code was on her smartphone. She pushed the button and at first felt nothing. Her heart pounded, and she felt a smile come across her face. It was an odd sensation, the smiling, but then she felt a little light-headed.

"More likely, it will take milliseconds to download, but I am experiencing some lightness, as if I were out of breath." Sage was about to continue until she saw her specialist seemingly slump in his chair. His eyes closed, and his head dipped to the left.

"No, no, no—what's happening to you, Mr. Cobb?" While still clutching her smartphone, Sage was up and putting her hands on her colleague to see what was wrong. As soon as she touched him, however, she felt a shock, stronger than any static or alternating current she had ever experienced before. As if completing an arc, a strong electrical current ran right through her. Even as she felt the ground rush to her face, she had the image of her touching Cobb as completing an electrical output arch, and now she was charged.

CHAPTER SEVEN

Cobb woke up to see that Sage had fallen into his lap. With her face and head on him as he sat, he was both surprised and embarrassed at the same time. Then he remembered passing out and her falling on him after some massive shock. He placed his hands on her shoulders and guided her limp body to the floor with ease. She was light, and his chairs were already close to the floor. Although it typically was a struggle to get out of the chairs, this time, the chairs' proximity to the ground was a good thing.

He laid her out on the floor and then rubbed his head. His office seemed dark, as if it was twilight. He checked her pulse and her breathing, and both seemed normal.

"What the hell happened here?" He looked around his office; everything seemed in place, but it was dark. It was as dark as if passing thunderstorm clouds had blotted out the sun. He looked outside through the open blinds.

"Have we been out for hours?" he said. He was already moving and was pulling the blinds up with the cord when he noticed that the darkness was unusual. It was a strange darkness, a twilight that he had seen once before, years ago, when he was in St. Louis for a trauma conference. His mind's eye recalled the darkness of a total solar eclipse in August 2017, a peachy dusk that produced no shadows.

Back then, it was a time of political and global upheaval—an abrasive, divisive businessman was president, North Korea was threatening nuclear war with functioning ICBMs, California was nearly consumed by wildfires, a record number of hurricanes had submerged three states and Puerto Rico, China was on the verge of a massive pandemic, and Germany was becoming a rising force, again.

But it was that total eclipse that he remembered well. It happened in North America, where he and millions of others witnessed the path of totality; several states experienced complete darkness when the moon blocked out the sun. He remembered the land being eerily silent as a gradual though dramatic decrease in sunlight eventually created darkness in midday. And when he had looked up to see the corona of the sun and the moon's Bailey's beads in all their other-worldliness, the image of a bullet in the sun came to mind as the best descriptor. Now, with the blinds completely retracted and minutes of blinking his eyes and looking out on the empty parking lot and dark landscape, Cobb found himself seeing the exact same image he saw on August 21, 2017. He had missed the last one in April 2024, but he assumed it was as amazing as the great American eclipse he had seen.

"It can't be," he said. "That was years ago. The next one isn't for years to come."

He spoke aloud to make sure he was not hallucinating. Cobb then pulled out his own smartphone to call James and Jennifer, but his fully charged phone was now dead, as if it had been out of charge for days. He felt suddenly hot. Still in his full three-piece suit, he took his jacket off and loosened his tie, leaving him with a still-intact vest, shirt, and slacks. He moved next to the landline phone and attempted to call the operator, then security, hoping to get an outside line for emergency services or to at least see if his children were safe. Nothing—no dial tone, no answers, no sounds; it was as if the phone line had been cut. When he checked to make sure and saw that it hadn't, it made him more anxious.

He stared back at the nonmoving total solar eclipse, which hung in the dark sky with its bright corona, as if it were stuck. He stood still and watched. He looked at his watch repeatedly. It was stopped, frozen at 11:45 a.m. His internal clock told him that five minutes or so had passed, and then he remembered that his client was on the floor and that he needed to get help. He forced himself to move and headed out to the common hall to get water and assistance from other therapists and support staff. He had expected the hall to be illuminated with fluorescent light, but it was dark. He looked to the left and right and could see that the normally closed therapy doors were open, and the limited eclipsed light filled their windows. He went up and down to each office to see if anyone was there. There was no one. He was alone.

"This is insane. What the hell is going on?"

He moved to the support staff office, which was typically teeming with administrative assistants, computer monitors all aglow with data, figures, and client records. It was as empty and as dark as the other offices. Upon closer inspection, he realized that in addition to the lack of people, the darkness, and the emptiness, there were no sounds at all—no landline phones ringing or blinking, no wall clocks ticking, no ever-present hum of electricity and not even the emergency exit signs were glowing. He picked up the phone and tried many lines, the intercom, and the public announcement system, and still, there was no sound. Attempts to operate the computers met with the same results: nothing.

"Blackout," he said. He moved to the back of the office. As he went to get water for his client, he saw that just like the offices in his wing, the same was true for the other side, where the staff lounge was housed. Although there was some low light coming in from the street, he had to move slowly, now balancing two cups of water, for the return trip to his office. He had made sure to bring two cups for his client. He had consumed three while he was there, and his dry, parched mouth was still devoid of saliva.

Even with a blackout, where are the people?

In short order, he had made it back to his office to see that his client was no longer on the floor. His heart skipped a beat until he saw her looking outside, mesmerized—like he must have been earlier—by what she saw outside the window. A total solar eclipse was amazing; a frozen total solar eclipse held fast in time was simply alien.

"Melanie?" he said in as close to a therapeutic, calming voice as he could muster.

She cried out, startled, as she whipped around to see who was there.

"It's me—Robert Cobb!"

After a second, she caught her breath and seemed to recognize him.

Without hesitation, he came to her with water. Some water had spilled on his leg. It didn't matter at the moment.

CHAPTER EIGHT

Sage was alone in the office when she awoke. She remembered seeing her counselor slump in his chair, as if he were having a grand mal seizure, then feeling a current run through her body when she went to his side and touched him. The shock upon contact threw her off-balance, and she thought she had landed on top of him, but when she found herself flat on her back in a dark room with a total solar eclipse frozen above a darkened, frightening landscape, she thought she was dead. She had left the office briefly to see that the building was dark and devoid of life before returning to her place in front of the window, peering at an astronomically impossible sight. She had also looked at her smartphone, only to find it was completely out of charge. So deep in thought as to what had happened and what to do next, she had not heard anyone behind her until someone called her name. She screeched, startled out of her hypnotic state.

"I'm so sorry I startled you," Cobb said.

Sage had an overwhelming desire to hug him but saw he had two cups in his hand, so that would have been difficult to do, maybe socially inappropriate as well.

"I'm sorry I screamed. What's happening, Mr. Cobb? I mean, look at that," she said and pointed out the window.

"Here, Melanie, drink this. It's water. I found I was dry when I saw all of this."

She reached for the water and took a sip at first, but then she realized she really was thirsty and drank the whole cup. Cobb handed her another, which was not filled as much, but it was good since she finished that one too. She breathed in and out through her nose to calm herself down. It was a great technique that Mr. Cobb had taught her, and neuroscience and the practical results supported its validity.

"Melanie, I have no idea how or what is happening. I just know none of this is right. A solar eclipse lasts minutes, and this has been going on for at least ten or more. And I found no one around—it's as if there's a blackout or something," Cobb said.

"A blackout shouldn't affect my smartphone," she said.

"My phone is dead too, and my watch stopped at 11:45 a.m. I have no idea," he added.

Sage found herself running through multiple scenarios, each one wilder than the last. She was thinking about the mathematical possibility of both of them slipping into some alternative universe. It was the thinking that her assistant Paula Dirac would have come to faster. Sage was wondering if it really was possible when Cobb interrupted her thinking with a logical idea.

"I've checked all the offices and both wings. I'm not crazy about this idea, but maybe we should go outside and see what's happening. I haven't seen any cars, headlights, people, or trains from here. It's always busy with traffic and activity, and there's just nothing out there."

"You're right. Maybe there's something we're not seeing. Let's go," Sage said. She felt a little bit better with a course of action, and it was an action she was familiar with: when in doubt, collect more data.

"OK. Just so you know, I have never been this confused in my life," Cobb said. She wondered why he had said what he did but then appreciated that it sounded honest, as it was accurate for her as well.

"Me too. I have no idea how any of this could happen, and there's nothing in my experience or anything I have ever come across to yield this," she said as she pointed to the fixed eclipse.

"OK, then, let's go," he said. He opened a drawer in his desk and took out his car keys. She wasn't sure where they might be going, but driving could be necessary to find someone fast if the research building in the navy yard was as empty and as strange as this building, which was just outside of the yard.

Cobb extended his hand and led the way. She was reluctant at first but then concluded that he worked in the building and would be the better choice to navigate the dark hallways.

It was slow going, as the interior hallways had no access to windows until beyond the exit, where they spilled into an open foyer with floor-to-ceiling glass.

"You have no idea what's happening? Did you download something from your smartphone?" Cobb asked as they walked slowly through the darkness.

"I uploaded a new code to my brain implant to enhance cognitive processing. I'm guessing by what happened that you have one too—an older one that's not insulated?"

"You're right. Mine helps with mood stabilizing. You sure you didn't create a time machine or portal into an alternative universe?"

Sage couldn't tell if he was joking or not, but she had already run through that most unlikely scenario and came up with nothing.

"I had those thoughts and crazier ones, but I just don't think I stumbled across that invention. I really just introduced what I thought were some minor codes and algorithms, and here is where we are—wherever 'here' is," she said.

There was a brief silence before Sage felt the urge to blurt out her fear, which she kept thinking was the most likely situation.

"Maybe we're dead."

She felt Cobb slow his pace just a little bit but then pick it up a moment later.

"I thought that, too, but why would we experience the same thing? I thought some kind of hallucination, but then, how does this place exist for both of us? I'm not a specialist on death and the afterlife, but I thought death, like birth, is a one-person trip and not a shared experience."

"Unless you're a twin or triplets."

"OK, maybe the birth thing is an exception—but death? And do twins and triplets remember womb time together, anyway?"

There was a brief silence again, and then they made it to the exit. The door opened; the view of the dark exterior via total solar eclipse that was now probably thirty minutes in duration was all that lit the open space of glass. Both of them walked down the stairs. Cobb had released her hand, as there was dim light for her to navigate. Without hesitation, she was the first to push open the door and stand outside the building, with Cobb right behind her.

She stood still, looked all around, and listened. The dark outline of Boston's skyline was bathed in the eerie light of the darkened sun. The air was still, but just as strange was the lack of traffic noise, planes, or anything else. The air was still warm, as it was summer, but it felt cooler because it was devoid of complete sun.

"This is crazy . . . no sound, no lights, no birds or people. I've never seen anything like this," Cobb said.

"Unbelievable," she said.

Cobb walked toward the parking lot with his keys already out. She followed and watched him point his remote-entry device at what was presumably his car, to no avail. After just a few attempts as he walked, he focused and found the key. He opened it, and there was no sound of door chimes, no interior light to illuminate the cabin. With the door still open, he got behind the wheel, pushed the key into the ignition, and turned it. There was just a click, then nothing. There was no stalling, no sputtering turnover, nothing but clicks as he tried turning the engine on. He then got out and moved to the trunk of the car and rummaged through one of many compartments until he pulled out two flashlights. Sage felt just a glimmer of hope, but similar to the car, no beams of light emerged. He tossed the flashlights back into the trunk and shut it.

"Nothing, no batteries or electricity, no sun, no noise, no people, nothing," Cobb said. He leaned against the car trunk and looked as if he was thinking. Sage turned and looked in the direction of the research building and pointed.

"There are backup generators and other possible power sources plus a shortwave radio. We should give that a try," she said.

Cobb looked in the direction of where she pointed and nodded.

"Good idea. I'm betting the Naval Research Department should have a little more than I would have in my trunk," he said. Cobb stood up and smoothed his vest down over his shirt and tie and then waved her to lead the way.

"All right, let's see what we can find in my place," she said.

"I hope we have better luck there."

"Me too," she said, although logically she was having a hard time understanding anything that was happening, and if electrical and battery-operated devices didn't work, nothing in the building would work either. She hoped the walk over might help her think of something.

CHAPTER NINE

Cobb was very tired. He and Sage had been in almost every office, cubicle, closet, and even the "off-limits" security areas, which were all open. If there were backup protocols for keeping secret places secret, they were all shut down. In the hours of walking, exploring, and trying to find clues as to what was happening, he had learned just a couple of things: there was no power—electrical, battery, mechanical, or engine. There was no sign of animal life, whether it be human, bird, mouse, dog, cat, absolutely nothing except vegetation like grass, trees, and indoor plants. And adding to the insanity, the solar eclipse had been hanging above the landscape for hours.

Then he noticed another strange thing: everything was pulled together in an orderly fashion. The only thing disheveled and lived-in was his clothes, which were sweaty and rumpled, reflecting his growing fatigue. After climbing some more stairs, he and his companion looked out a third-story window of the crypt-like research building; from this vantage point, he could see that the streets were clear of cars and trucks—they were all neatly parked along the road as if the city was set up for a movie stage. The building's interior was also perfectly arranged, with chairs pushed into their desks and no coffee cups or stray magazines out of place. He looked back at the perfectly arranged sea of workstations and then back outside just to fully embrace the oddity. The entire building, the whole city, everything within sight was set in place and staged as if it were all a lifelike dollhouse. It certainly had none of the chaos and messiness of a lived-in world.

"Things look so orderly. Everything looks like it has a place. It's as if it were all staged, like it was all put into place to receive people. It's so strange," Sage said. She was standing beside him, looking out the third-floor window over Boston Harbor, a dark cityscape, and empty roads bathed in the alien and celestial coronal light.

"I wish I could even guess at what it all means, what's going on. Being dead sounds more and more likely. I really can't—"

"I don't think I would smell of old sweat and be so tired," Cobb cut in.

Cobb's thoughts were interrupted by a series of flashes that lit up the dark sky with what looked like a series of letters, numbers, and symbols; some seemed familiar, but others did not. The stream of flashes moved across the dark sky quickly, as if it were streaming on an invisible screen.

"What is that?" Cobb was at a loss. When he heard nothing, he turned to see that Sage was transfixed by the flashing data.

"Melanie? What is that? Have you seen that before?" Cobb asked.

"It's code . . . a command computer code," she said without emotion, never taking her gaze off the patch of sky that was expanding with both familiar and strange symbols and letters. "It's some kind of command computer program that's flashing across the sky. It's as if we're watching a computer screen while someone writes or generates code," Sage said. Her volume was low, and she stood transfixed.

As suddenly as it had appeared, it vanished.

"What? Where did it go?" Cobb asked.

He didn't hear Sage's response. In a flash, the darkness of the solar eclipse vanished, and the sun appeared low on the horizon, as if it were close to sunset. The relatively bright light temporarily blinded him, leaving him blinking wildly so that he could refocus his vision.

"That was some kind of code. It's as if someone just input data, changing whatever was happening before. But it can't be. I mean, we're not in a computer. This is the real world, right?" he heard Sage say.

It took under a minute for his sight to adjust to the new lighting. He still couldn't see any people or signs of life outside, but he swore there was now snow on the ground.

"Is . . . is that snow? Weren't we still in summer a couple of seconds ago?" Cobb said.

As he looked at the ground, he felt the floor tremble underneath his feet. It was a clear tremor but not like an earthquake; it was too quick and short, as if it were a step. Just a moment later, there was another one, then another.

"Those are footsteps," Sage said. Cobb was impressed by her lack of emotion. He knew the tremors were footsteps, but he was genuinely frightened about what could produce such shaking. It didn't take him long to find the owner. Its size was enormous, maybe six stories tall and broad. It was bipedal, completely covered with some kind of scales, and had four massive arms that ended in claws. It seemed to move with purpose and then came to a dead stop blocks away and looked at the ground. It screeched at whatever it was looking at, and then it was hit with a series of beams. The creature screeched again and backed away. The sources of the beams appeared to be large black and orange orbs that were as big as buses, but they hovered as if they were hummingbirds while shooting some beam that was hurting the creature. The creature was not passively accepting the punishing beams; its four massive arms picked up the parked vehicles that were at its feet and hurled them as if they were toys at the converging orbs. With a total of five orbs hovering and adjusting their flight patterns, two were hit and exploded upon impact, and another was grazed and seemed to crash to the ground. A fireball confirmed it was not a gentle landing. The explosions were also forceful enough to shake the building and the glass of the window they were watching from. The two remaining orbs moved farther away, and the creature retreated in the other direction. The tremors of its footsteps indicated it was leaving—making good distance as the shaking subsided. The orbs continued firing and followed the creature.

Cobb watched the retreating orbs until they were out of sight.

He looked at Sage, who returned his gaze and looked back to where the explosion of the crashed orb had started a fire in two brick buildings.

"What the hell is all of this?" Sage said. Unlike last time, her voice was elevated. The volume was enough to pull his attention back and focus on her. He had no idea what was going on—some massive alien creature from a nightmare and attacking orange orbs that fired beams that burned and exploded upon impact. None of it made sense.

More letters, numbers, and symbols appeared in bright yellow upon a light-blue sunset and fire below, and then they disappeared.

"I don't know," Cobb said. He moved away from the window and was startled by the sudden appearance of fluorescent lights flickering on and the internal array of electrical and computer equipment coming to life. Panning left and right, he saw that ghostlike figures were moving around in purposeful and deliberate fashion. At first there was no noise, but as the specters solidified, so did the ambient noise of a very busy command center filled with multiple computer stations and people in dark-green, blue, and black vests over black battlefield dress uniforms. All had sidearms and were obviously busy with some kind of emergency.

"Please tell me you see this," Cobb said into her ear.

"Yes, I do, but this isn't what the research departments are like."

"So this isn't some kind of secret military place?"

"No. We're all civilians. This was a work area, nonmilitary for the most part. Some officers at times, but nothing like this," Sage said.

"Dr. Sage? Mr. Cobb? Where have you been? And why aren't you in uniform?" a strong, authoritative voice boomed out at them. Cobb followed the voice to a tall, blonde-haired, blue-eyed woman in a dark-green vest, similar battle dress uniform, and side arm. She was accompanied by her own similarly dressed security team, but they wore maroon vests.

Cobb knew the woman, but Sage called her by name.

"Doctor Karlsson? I'm confused. What's going on, and why should I be in uniform?"

Dr. Karlsson appeared confused by the question and then narrowed her eyes in anger.

"Dr. Sage, we're at war with those things out there, and I have no time for this. Mr. Cobb, I sent her to you to get her head back in the game, and you both come back here walking around like you're civilians on your way to a coffee shop. What are you both thinking?"

It was easy to see she was annoyed. The confrontation ended quickly when both his children, James and Jennifer, arrived with a series of other soldiers, all wearing black and in various conditions of health. All were heavily armed, and his two adult children looked angular, hard, and very old, as if they had been toughened by years of conflict. He had seen it in his veteran clients but never his children. There was scarring on his son's face, and his daughter's right arm was clearly a mechanical replacement, devoid of aesthetic covering for maximum functionality.

"James? Jennifer?" Cobb said.

His son came to a stop a foot from him and the group while his daughter shot past her brother and gave her father a hug. She held him tight, and he could feel both her equipment and strong muscles. Her hair smelled of sweat, oil, smoke, and gunpowder. Jennifer had always been less affectionate, was soft rather than muscled, and had a thing with smelling good and spending hours on her hair.

"Christ, Dad. We heard grid RD 45 was hit and got here as soon as we could." His son stopped and took another look at him. "And what the hell are you wearing?"

"You scared the shit out of me and Mom, Dad. What were you thinking?" Jennifer said while she hugged him. He looked at his son as he held his daughter. He took in his son's chiseled features, military buzz cut, and the deep scar that went from his right eye down his cheek to his chin.

"Jennifer . . . James . . ."

His daughter's hug faded rapidly, along with all the sights, sounds, people, and everything else that was alive at that moment.

"No! Where are you? Where did you go?"

Cobb looked around a darkening open floor with desks, tables, and stations all off again, in perfect positioning, with no electricity or people. He looked around and saw that it was once again Sage and him alone in an empty room. He looked outside, and the destruction from the crashed orb, the creatures, and the prior battle was nonexistent, as if it had never happened.

He moved away from the window and sat at a nearby computer station that was like all the others, dark, empty, and silent. Sage seemed to give him a little space. He appreciated her giving him time to process the images of his adult children, who had materialized before his eyes and then disappeared within minutes. The horizon over the dark, lightless cityscape was slowly being illuminated by a rising full moon.

"Are you all right, Mr. Cobb?"

He took a moment before he answered.

"I am. It was just hard to see my kids, looking like weary soldiers, and then have them disappear."

There was more silence. He turned to see what Sage was doing. She was still looking at him, and then she spoke.

"Just as you were hugging, there was another series of symbols and code in the sky. As soon as it flashed off, everything evaporated, just like before."

Cobb nodded as if it all made sense. It didn't, but there was a pattern—whenever the writing and symbols appeared, something in their world changed.

"You may be right, Melanie. Maybe that's code, and we're a computer program."

CHAPTER TEN

In the time it took to walk the fourteen city blocks to his children's apartment, there had been one more set of coding in the sky, and it appeared as if it were lunchtime in Boston proper in the summer. Everything was as it might normally be, except nearly everyone was wearing photo-sensitive visual devices or glasses and seemed to be completely immersed in activities or conversations and busy with everything but still navigating the streets without banging into each other. The next obvious thing was that there were no vehicles at all on the streets. The streets were filled with people; nearly all were casually dressed, as if on holiday, and no professional types in suits to be seen. Sage had the unusual experience of feeling overdressed and conspicuous; she was disheveled, with low athletic body odor, but still far from casual.

She watched Cobb try to engage people passing by, but they moved on as if he was not even there. She could see them avoid him and her, so she deduced that they were visible to the people but that they were just not engaging because they were involved in whatever they were seeing or doing with their glasses.

Sage also noticed another thing: in the series of events that occurred with the changing programs, her smartphone came back on with power. Although it was fully juiced, it would be depleted when there was a change. It always picked up at 11:45 a.m. After just three changes, she had narrowed the amount of time she needed to upload the application to her brain.

After about twenty minutes, when they were a block away from Cobb's children's home, the code appeared again, and everything returned to its staged, empty appearance; all the vehicles had returned, but they were parked and still, with no electricity or sounds.

She had repeated the uploading procedure, but nothing happened. Five minutes had passed in silence when she realized that she missed something. She had not been in physical contact with Cobb.

Is that what's necessary? Physical contact? Maybe biometric contact was a way of linking two brains or organic computers in this case.

"Maybe we're dead after all?" Cobb asked. She could tell it was a genuine question. She had already ruled that out as a possibility and was off to engaging other lines of thinking, from alternative universes to string theory.

"Mr. Cobb, I have a crazy theory, but it's one that might make the most sense."

"Well, since I keep coming up with being dead, I'm open to ideas. What do you think is going on?"

"It's going to sound crazy," she warned.

Sage heard Cobb first chuckle, and then he laughed aloud. His pace did not falter, and he kept heading in a specific direction, but his laughter continued even in the eeriness of an empty metropolitan city with no noise. Once she was beyond the sound of his laughter, she realized that her "crazy" theory was probably more reasonable than what they had experienced so far.

"Well, I bet it will make more sense than a solar eclipse that lasts for twenty minutes and six-limbed creatures six stories tall fighting laser beam machines that hover over an empty city."

Sage felt herself smile as well. It was the only humor she had found in the day so far.

She saw Cobb slow his pace down and then look at a door. His laughter gone, it was evident he was experiencing something else. Confusion?

"This is the right number and right place, but the door is black. It was a God-awful orange door before," he said. She watched him hesitate for a moment more, and then he opened the door, and she followed him in. The hall was dark, as there were no lights, just shafts of light coming in from the skylight seven flights up and small windows that appeared on every landing. By the time she caught up with Cobb, he was standing in the middle of a large apartment room with a row of computer workstations, four in all, that were powerless and dark. She found it odd that there was nothing else in the room except for the stations and old-style beanbags dropped at different places. There was no furniture or media or entertainment areas—there was nothing that would imply it was the home of two adult children. Cobb was checking other areas of the spacious apartment while she looked at the computer setup, multiple screens and very high-end CPUs cobbled together to get way more power than what was on the market for private use.

"Other than it being clean, dark, and quiet, it looks the way it should, except no one is here, just like everywhere else," Cobb said. His look was that of seriousness and concern.

"Well, they're not here," he added.

Sage nodded. If it was like everything else she had experienced that day, his children would not be there unless another program was run.

"They were the young man and woman in uniform," Sage said.

"Yup. They were never in the military. They played military games online for money and did well, but they were not very athletic, let alone the seasoned, battle-hardened soldiers I saw back there."

"They looked like they were veterans for sure," Sage said.

There was a moment of silence. Sage watched Cobb look around the empty room, and then he looked back at her.

"So, Melanie, you have a theory?"

CHAPTER ELEVEN

"Well, that's interesting," Cobb said. He was surprised at how calm he was and how Sage's theory didn't seem to bother him. As the hours had passed and he had run through every possible explanation of what was happening, this one explanation seemed the more plausible.

By now, they had left his children's building and were heading back to where it all began for him.

"So there are entire theories on this as an explanation for our existence? That life is just a simulation—we're part of some computer program?" Cobb asked.

Before he could answer, more numbers appeared, and their environs changed again. This time, it was something familiar. Everything looked as if it were the 1970s, and for the first time in both this adventure and recent years, he saw other men wearing three-piece suits similar to his and others dressed in that same period wardrobe. All the sights, smells, and sounds were mid-1970s.

Cobb was about to say more but saw that Sage was already on her phone while she had power. She kept up with him but was focused on her phone. He kept with her to make sure that no one banged into her so that she could complete her work. It was hard to keep her from hitting passersby and hard for him not to be distracted by a vivid re-creation of a bygone period.

The minutes passed, and it was taking a little longer to get back to his office when a vaguely familiar man came right up to him. He was a tall, younger man, maybe in his early thirties, with dark hair and piercing brown eyes. He knew the smile, expression, and eyes, but he could not place the person at all. When the stranger spoke, it was familiar in tone, pitch, and volume. The content was also something he had heard before.

"Well, I should have known I would find you here. You know, you look good for an old man. I look better, I bet."

Cobb waited and took his time. Everything was familiar to him except one thing: this Dr. Paul Gerson had to be thirty years younger than the last time he saw him.

"Paul? Paul Gerson? Is that you? Really?" Cobb's voice went dry. He looked at Sage to make sure she was seeing what he was seeing; it was obvious that she was also experiencing the same events.

"How is this possible?" Cobb asked.

"I got to be brief, so here were go. Your friend here is right," Dr. Gerson said with a nod to Sage. "Everything you experience in 'life' is a simulation. It's more than that, much more, but I can best put it in these terms, as it will more likely make the most sense to you."

"What do you mean?" The man had Cobb and Sage's undivided attention in the middle of a 1970s afternoon on the streets of Boston, Massachusetts.

It was easy to see that this man was a young Dr. Gerson; his mannerisms, smile, tendency to overexplain, and appearance, right down to the awful tie and nonmatching suit, were all characteristic of him, but Cobb had never known Dr. Gerson as a young man.

"All right, Bob, work with me here," Dr. Gerson said as he took a step closer to Cobb and Sage, with pedestrians moving all around them.

The phrase "work with me" was one of his usual sayings.

"Here's the short version. Forget heaven and hell, but think conservation of energy. We die, and the body stops, but our memories, dreams, and what we call identity are all uploaded into a human memory cloud, like when you used to talk about having all of your computer data stored outside of your computer."

"A virtual storage drive where all individual entities, humans, when we die, our essence or soul is sent," Sage said.

"Oh, I see you're not just a pretty face," Gerson said with a chuckle.

"And energy can't be completely destroyed, but it can transition, mutate, or convert to something else," she said.

"Correct, but there's more. Your thoughts, feelings, and experiences—everything you do is not just your point of view; when you sleep, all of that is uploaded into a shared consciousness. It is that shared consciousness that you return to when you die," he added.

Cobb felt suddenly tired, and then he felt as if the most complex thing had been simply explained.

"So there's not an afterlife like we think of it but a transition to something," Cobb said with obvious struggle.

"Come on, Bob, you had to know that the amount of time and vulnerability that sleep incurs would have been a crazy evolutionary step unless it had a major purpose," Gerson said.

"So what you're saying is that in a similar vein, our lives are endured, then uploaded to a massive stream of consciousness in the form in which we all end up? And this is why we sleep? To transmit what we experienced? These reiterations of life, these simulations we have been experiencing—" Sage was saying when Dr. Gerson interrupted.

"They are all programs that are running all the time in different phases, at different points that are all real to the viewer and powered by past minds. That's why you have strong feelings about some things, people whom you have never met but you already feel you know, the feeling of familiarity and déjà vu, universal themes such as love, hate, jealousy, and all of those things you 'just know' and what you might call as instinct or intuition—all of these things are familiar to you because you're tied in with the greater consciousness, the great 'cloud' in the sky."

As they stood in the cityscape of more than seventy years ago, Cobb experienced a palpable silence. Everything Gerson said seemed to make some sense to him, but his much smarter colleague seemed to embrace the concepts entirely.

"But once in a great while, we get some smartass that comes from one lower level of consciousness and gets a peep into a higher level," Gerson said. Again, he pointed his head in the direction of Sage.

"All near-death experiences make the trip, but we can keep them from accessing much, but then you get some whose brain somehow taps it all—like Einstein, Hawking, Fermi, Shelley, Bostrum, and a whole bunch of others."

"That could explain how things in life really go crazy at times, like the 2016 presidential elections, the great 2017 hurricanes, and global warming, and why light has both wave and particle attributes. It's as if it were all part of a sophisticated computer program with errors and divergent codes at times," Sage added.

Dr. Gerson's smile broadened in his customary way that Cobb remembered seeing when he got something right, like a more complicated diagnosis.

"Like I said, some have gotten here, and others have tapped into the greater mind cloud, but I have to say, though, this is the first time someone has artificially engaged the transit here. You've got some serious skills, Dr. Sage."

Gerson's presentation was just as Cobb had remembered, right down to his idioms and expressions.

"How do you know about me? You know Mr. Cobb—but me?"

"I'm about two levels up from where you are in the experience you call 'life.' I can look into the past like a book while your experience is being written about for the book, still in progress, which could go left or go right, which leads me to another important thing before I go."

Cobb found himself cringing at the thought of his friend leaving. Gerson looked up to the sky. Cobb followed his gaze and saw more numbers and letters streaming over a beautiful blue sky with fewer buildings in the Boston skyline.

"The more full and interesting life you have, the more you share and contribute to the collective consciousness, and the more fulfilling your future leveled-up time will be," Gerson said.

Cobb was sure he heard the words but wasn't 100 percent sure what he meant. His expression must have conveyed the confusion as Dr. Gerson spoke again before everything fluttered out.

"Make sure you have interesting lives and live to your fullest. The more you do here, the more you get when you die. The more energy released from your brain—memories, experiences, thinking—and the more you leave behind, the more you will have when you join us. Otherwise, if you don't, you really will be deleted, gone, and finished. That would be bad."

The words lingered as the 1970s world receded into the background and then disappeared completely. The world was again empty, devoid of people, movement, and sound, as if all were put in storage, cleared, and checked until it was called upon again to stage another event.

"Shit, that was a lot," Cobb heard Sage say.

CHAPTER TWELVE

"Well, I'm glad we're here instead of out there," Sage said.

The sounds of insects crawling toward them through the closed windows were ominous. There were soldiers at the ready—men and women clothed in smooth, tight-fitting uniforms separated by colors of red, blue, black, and red—with sophisticated carbines all poised to shoot an incoming swath of bugs, which looked like ants as big as cats and made loud clicking noises. These hideous creatures were crawling over themselves and getting through the barriers that would trigger the fire of the defenders. The barriers of burned-out, modern-style military vehicles looked as if they were hastily put in place, probably as a last line of defense before the shooting started. Sage and Cobb had been in his office when the code flashed across the sky, and Sage launched into her program again. She was glad that it was done and that they were not still outside—hopefully, they wouldn't be there for very long.

"All this looks horrible. Do you think it's going to work? You think we'll be able to leave here and all these in-between worlds?" Cobb asked. It was easy to see he was tired and overwhelmed. What started out as an interesting night and a clinical session had evolved into a greater understanding of the world and the very essence of existence.

"That was pretty heady stuff Dr. Gerson said; being deleted sounds bad."

"Funny, I used to think that dying would be bad, but it sounds like there's a whole lot more that could be out there."

"As long as we do interesting things here and live to our fullest. Any idea what that means?" Sage asked.

"I don't know—maybe help others, do more things, and have children. I guess be able to look back and say, 'Shit, that was a pretty interesting life,' and have few to no regrets. One thing's for sure, the proverb of 'when the game is over, the king and the pawn go to the same place' might not be true."

Sage made one more adjustment she thought important. In her distracted focus, the quote flashed before her inner eye. "'When the game is over, the king and the pawn go into the same box.' An Italian proverb and I get your point. I guess that's not all true."

"For sure, it kind of gives you hope for the journey to continue."

Sage had been thinking a lot, racing thoughts, really, since their interaction with Cobb's friend. She had never heard it—life, death, and beyond—so logically and simply put. Still, she was emotionally fatigued and felt tired and very hungry. She could feel old sweat and smell her body odor; her body felt stretched out and exhausted. Cobb smelled better, although his tie was gone, and his usually calm demeanor looked fatigued and disheveled.

She felt that all that had transpired had aged her, and by the looks of Cobb, it had done the same thing to him as well. Still, she was invigorated by the whole experience. She had a couple of questions, but she felt like she had more answers than she ever would have imagined.

"I should have known the energy needs to go somewhere when you die. And sleeping—how could I miss that?" she said.

Sage didn't wait for an answer but instead pressed her powered-up smartphone, launched the app, and took Cobb's hand. What he might have misconstrued as giving comfort was the missing part of getting back—back to the familiar, his reality, his level, where it all started for the both of them.

I hope this works. Will I remember everything?

There was a shock, light-headedness, and then a burning sensation. She turned to see what was happening to Cobb, but she was already fading, and then she was feeling the ground rush to her face.

~

The first thing Cobb noticed was that he was in a sitting position. His mouth was as dry as if he had run a marathon, and his body felt so tired, it took effort to open his eyes. At first, his vision was blurry, and the light seemed too bright for him to see anything. While mere seconds felt like minutes, he remembered that the brilliant June day was kept at bay by the blinds. Still, the warm rays penetrated and lit up his office. As his eyes adjusted, he shifted in his low chair. He felt fatigued and was surprised to find his jacket still on over his charcoal vest, matching slacks, and dress shirt and tie. Upon closer inspection, however, his jacket appeared perfectly dry-cleaned and pressed in comparison to the rest of his attire, which looked as if he had spent hours or longer walking, running, or doing something physically active.

"I know, Mr. Cobb, my armpits smell, and I feel as bad as I look," he heard Sage say.

He had forgotten to check on her at first because he was so focused on himself. He looked her over, and it was true: it looked like she, too, had been active, and her hair, similar to his, was disheveled, and there were circles under her eyes. He started to say something but needed a second to clear his throat before he spoke.

"What . . . what do you remember? Was I asleep?"

Cobb watched her sit up a little straighter in the low chair. He could see it took her effort. She looked to her right and then left and spoke without looking at him.

"Your friend Dr. Gerson had some advice about living life fully so as to 'level up.' The last place we were at looked like an invasion of giant ants against color-coded soldiers. There was a time when we saw some massive creature fight orbs, and then my boss and your children materialized in some kind of alternative military state. All of that sound familiar?"

Cobb felt his breath come up a little short, and then he forced himself to take a deeper breath before responding.

"So it was real. All of it?" he said. He was staring at her and saw her look down at the space between them. Lying on the floor between them was her smartphone. It was vibrating, and the digital clock glowed in large white letters against a bright-blue backdrop screen of sky and sun. It was on and showing the time. It was a mere ten minutes into their session.

He took his time to pull up more saliva before he spoke again.

"Well, I don't know whether you should pick it up, but if you do, I'll stay over here."

Without a word, she pulled herself to the smartphone and picked it up. Although she was a younger woman, he heard her groan as if she had extended herself and was aching. He was not surprised, however, that she scooped it up and then put it right into her pocket. She then stood up and extended her hands to help him up.

"Ah, no offense, but in light of the last time we touched, I think I'll pull myself up." Saying it was a lot easier than doing it. He was nonetheless up and now faced her. He could see she was distracted, but at the same time, she seemed thoughtful.

"Well . . . that was the longest and shortest session I have ever experienced," he said.

"Yes . . . Mr. Cobb? I want to thank you for all your work and the insights you have assisted me with over the past year. It has been a learning experience, and this last session was . . . was life-altering. I think I have some things to do."

Cobb was not sure what to say, let alone about what had happened. They both had experienced something unusual that was real but fantastic. But he thought just a moment longer about what his mentor, Dr. Gerson, had said. Living a full and interesting life was something that would be important for the future life. It would result in leveling up, as if it was one of the games his son and daughter would play, progressing to ever-higher levels. The analogy was not lost on him.

"Are you leaving? Are you going to go off and do interesting things?"

"Interesting and meaningful things, things that really make a difference, that make changes and affect many things—all of the things I have to do if I want to go where Dr. Gerson and Einstein and Hawking went. Can you imagine?" she said with excitement and energy that emerged from thin air. Cobb couldn't help but smile. Her sudden newfound purpose was infectious. He wondered about his own future. He had kids, and he helped people. His smile faded as his mind fell on one question: *Is there more for me to do too?*

His expression must have spoken volumes. For the woman known for not reading facial cues, she nailed his.

"You have children and have affected many lives with your skills. I bet there's still more you could do if you think you need to."

Cobb could tell it was not just a thought but a legitimate question: *Have I done enough? Even if I have, is there more to do? Should I do more anyway?*

His thoughts leaped to seeing his old friend again. He was pulled back by Sage's taking up his right hand and shaking it.

"Thank you, Mr. Cobb, for everything."

"I think I have to thank you for your, ah, intervention, shall we say." He was not sure what he really wanted to say except that he got something, too, from her messing with her smartphone modification and his old radiofrequency-sensitive brain implant. He watched her smile and then turn to the closed door of his office, open it, and walk out. He had seen many people do that before, but she walked out taller than she had come in, more determined and focused than when she arrived. Still standing in front of his chair, he moved to the window and opened the blinds just a little to make sure it was still a sunny day in June. It was. Instead of closing it, he left them open and looked out. For the first time in a long time, he felt freer, less encumbered, and yet more resolute.

He looked out a moment longer before he took his jacket off and flung it on the chair he had vacated. He unbuttoned his suit vest to let his sweaty shirt cool off. He was not sure when his next appointment was coming, but he just needed a few more minutes alone to figure out the next steps for the rest of his life.

CHAPTER THIRTEEN

"So, you're coming in tomorrow? I'm not due for another two months," Melanie said. She knew that her mother's plans were already in motion, and convincing her otherwise would likely be impossible. Even over the patched cell-phone call, she could hear her mother moving about as if she were packing even as they spoke.

"This will give me time to see my two grandchildren and Paula," her mother said. "I haven't seen them in six months," she added.

"Which is the longest gap you have gone. Dad is probably regretting moving to Florida since you're always up here."

"Not remotely. He and John will go shooting and then golf for the entire period—"

"And that 'period' will be?" Sage interrupted.

"Well, four or five months, I would think."

"Four or five months? You'll live here again for four or five months? Mother! I didn't see you that much continuously when I lived with you."

"That's all right, Mel," a loud, kind voice interjected from the doorway. The former administrative assistant and doctoral student and now full-fledged doctor of theoretical mathematics was standing at the door of their bedroom suite.

Sage covered the phone, hoping her mother wouldn't hear.

"You want her to stay with us because she'll help with the babies, and you'll get to stay up all night with her playing cards and games. I swear, I should have had you marry her, and Dad could have moved in with me," she said in a hushed tone.

"That's entirely true," Paula said. Her smile was radiant even with her food-stained blouse and loose-fitting jeans. "And how often do spouses get along that well with their in-laws?" she asked.

"That's right," her mother said from the phone. It was painfully clear that her mother had heard everything her spouse said and was in full agreement, as always.

"Hi, Denise," Paula said, then added, "I'll get your room ready, and I'll hit the farmer's market for fresh apples. I've got to know how you make your apple pie. And I also have that walk-in bathtub set up out on the deck. It's like an outdoor Jacuzzi once it's all filled and running."

Sage pushed the speaker button on, lay down on her back, and placed the phone on her protruding, pregnant belly as if it were a table. She knew keeping her mother at bay was now impossible, and she went into damage-control mode of what could now be gained by her mother spending time with them. One thing came to mind, but she heard her mother talk first.

"No problem, Paula. It's really simple."

"No, figuring out the equations unifying the theoretical bases and context for coexisting universes and why light acts as both wave and particle in this universe is simple. Your apple pie's taste, texture, and smell are truly a mystery," Paula said. Even as she spoke, her gaze floated off as if she had solved those very riddles she actually was close to solving.

"Oh my God! You are such a dear!" Sage heard her mother say with glee.

Feeling as if she were twelve again, at the height of her lack of impulse control and inability to read social cues, Sage went right for what she wanted from the deal.

"All right, Mother; you can stay for the five months, and Paula can eat all the pie she wants, and you two can play games to your heart's content, but I want to be able to sleep and have sex with my betrothed, and that will require you staying up with your soon-to-be third grandchild."

"You got it," her mother said with zeal.

"And you," Sage said to Paula, "Don't get distracted from your work. Aren't you just shy of unifying the curvature of the universe as a variable of time? Kind of a big deal."

"Yes, yes, and it can wait for a few weeks so I can have a break with my favorite mother-in-law," she said.

"You see, Melanie, Paula knows what she's talking about," her mother said.

"Hmm," was all Sage said.

Rather than push further she continued to lie on her back and listen to more of the chatter. Her mother and Paula were not remotely upset by her blatant, frank demands about sex in their presence. Both women knew her too well to be embarrassed. As she looked at the ceiling, her mind wandered from the conversation and briefly touched upon how things had changed so quickly in five years: she was married to her best friend; had two three-year-old boys and a girl on the way; her wife was on the brink of making a massive contribution to mathematics, physics, and beyond; and she was experiencing such a full, fast-paced, never-stopping flood of experiences that she was convinced she had taken the right steps to "live an interesting life." While she was in the midst of it all and felt as if she had been forced to change, to be engaged outside of herself, and to add more to the world, she was feeling relief that when her time did come, she would "level up" and meet the great thinkers, world-shakers, and future builders of the other dimensions. Her heart felt lighter, and she could tell she was smiling as her hands rested on the sides of her belly.

A shadow came over her briefly as Paula lay down beside her.

"Now, where are your thoughts off to?" she asked.

Sage was surprised at first but then realized that she was daydreaming; the conversation between her mother and Paula had obviously concluded.

"I'm just thinking how happy I am with you and our life together."

The sentence came to her in an instant. It was true. Still, when she turned, she saw Paula tearing up.

"What did I say? Something wrong?" Sage felt worried for a moment, but when Paula smiled and used her warm hands to hold her face, she assessed that the tears might not be out of sadness or pain.

"That is the nicest thing anyone has ever said to me."

Sage reached out to touch Paula's face, and she felt herself smile again. Suddenly, the magnified sounds of babies moving came over the baby monitor. The monitor was sitting on the table feet away, but the sound was as if it were mere inches away from her ears.

"And the princes kill the moment again. I've got them. You nap, and I'll get you in an hour to start dinner," Paula said. She moved up and off the bed in seconds while Sage took all her strength to get up on her elbows. Before Paula was out the door, Sage called out to her just to make sure she knew she wasn't kidding about her demands.

"I'm serious about the sex thing when my mother comes. And it would be good for me later this week!"

"I'll take care of you, Princess," she heard Paula say from down the hall.

Next, she heard the animated conversation of her wife talking to their sons, who were nearly as verbal as she was to them.

Still resting on her elbows, lying on the bed, she looked out to the setting afternoon sun and smiled again.

"So another life really happens after this? That is so cool."

CHAPTER FOURTEEN

"OK, that's enough. You're fifty years old, and you're acting like a twenty-year-old," Jennifer said. Robert Cobb knew his daughter would see that he was only partially paying attention. It was clear he was focused on pulling together his gear for another cross-country trek to some disaster. Jennifer was far more intuitive and persistent than his son, James. He stopped himself to focus on her and her often-stated, differently phrased reasons why he should remain home and go back to counseling people in the office.

"You know, Jen, I liked it better when you made money playing video tournaments with your brother. You're so serious."

"Well, running a business will do that," she said. It was a response he had come to know held remorse and anger.

"I think you would be happier traveling and seeing the world. The dark suits and high heels have to hurt. And the annoying, entitled investors are far from pleasant, I'm sure," he added. His comment reminded him to bring his comfortable shoes and light Saharan clothing that had protection against UV rays. The fires in California in September were hot and dry once you got beyond the ash and heat. He would be with the Red Cross behind the fire lines, but that could easily change, like the time three years ago in Oregon.

He felt his daughter's eyes on him from behind, and he knew that her arms were crossed. He turned slowly, well-worn pants, vest, and shoes in his hands. He stopped and was eyeing the half-filled "go bag" he used for his out-of-state trips. He felt his shoulders slump and awaited the low-tone, logical argument that would be the beginning in an ongoing volley of points, counterpoints, and reasoning. Her eyes narrowed ever so slightly, one of her high heels dug into his floor, and her head tilted to the left.

"OK, go ahead," he said.

She wasted no time launching her first verbal strike. "I swear, Dad, the faster I mature and make these decisions, the more reckless you become. I've been worried about you for five years—this change in careers from therapist to Red Cross counselor. As soon as the shit hits and everyone tears out, you and those other crazies head into the mouth of disaster—"

"Once more unto the breach," Cobb quoted.

"Yes, I get that, but you've almost drowned in not one but two floods, you had to be the first crisis worker in the Halifax debris field after that explosion, and don't forget the series of fires in the West, hurricanes in Florida and on the Gulf Coast, and the only case of bubonic plague in modern US history in New Mexico. Your luck is going to run out, Dad."

Cobb listened to his daughter and understood her. All the near disasters and danger were real. Still, he had found his niche, a group of people who felt the same way, and they didn't have the advantage of knowing what he knew—the more interesting the life, the more likely an interesting and upgraded afterlife. His thoughts flickered to Melanie Sage, who had gotten married and had two boys to "make life interesting." And there was something her wife was working on too that was pretty big. He reminded himself he needed to call her. He had heard she was pregnant again.

"Are you even listening to me?" Jennifer said.

Cobb snapped back to the present and tried to focus on a rebuttal. It came faster than he expected.

"I know what I've been doing is not the usual course of action for an older guy—"

"You think? You're a father, and you should be taking it easy," she said.

"What do you mean 'taking it easy'? I was doing that, and it was a good gig, and I helped people. But what I do is helping people in crisis; it's being there when they really need someone, where few people go who really care. Don't you think that's a better thing? Do you hound Mum like this?"

"She's acting mature, and she's . . . doing what she likes."

"And we're different people; she loves golf, dinner on Wednesdays and Sundays, brunch on Mondays and Thursdays, and for the real big treats, it's a Mediterranean cruise. Do you really think that kind of life would be good for me? We figured that out decades ago."

He watched her think of a counterstrike. Her eyes shifted downward and left to right as if looking for some critical point she could develop in the moment.

"Come on, Jen. I'm a fifty-year-old guy who still has a lot of life left. I've lost so much weight that I'm off my blood pressure and cholesterol medicine, and I don't need my CPAP machine for sleeping anymore," he said. To prove his point, he turned his profile to her to display a leaner, fit version of himself. He would have pulled his T-shirt up to show his ribs and abdominal muscles, but his hands were still filled with his gear. He decided to use a little parental guilt.

"Do you really want me to be like my friends and your mother's friends? Do you think it's a good idea to slow down and go golfing? I really don't want to be that guy who fades away in a 'senior living' setting where I can watch the grass grow, complain about the sun or snow, and hope that either you or Jim will wipe my hairy ass when I can't."

"I'm not going to do that. I'll hire someone for that," she said matter-of-factly. It jarred Cobb a little that she had actually thought about that and had a plan. Still, he knew the speech was good, save for the very last part. He watched his daughter's jaw soften just a little, and her arms shifted to cross the other way while her high heel stopped digging into his hardwood floor. He remained still until she spoke. If it was Jim, the conversation would have been done, and he would have been out the door. He started to wonder where his ride was.

Finally, Jennifer sighed and uttered the words he knew she hated to say.

"All right. Go. But when you get back, we really have to find a more middle-of-the-road approach to what you're doing."

Cobb took her response as permission to get back to packing. He put his belongings in a solidly built backpack that was marked with several airline tags. The bright canary-yellow color made his bag easy for him to identify. He looked at his watch in one sweeping motion as he took his custom-packaged first-aid kit and an old set of throwing knives he kept in there as well for entertainment. He heard his daughter asking him more questions about logistics, schedules, and the level of danger—all questions he answered with ease while he moved to putting his field clothes together, which were clean for the moment but would not be within twenty-four hours.

He heard a horn honk, and by the sound of it, he was pretty sure who his ride was going to be. He felt the corners of his mouth curl up, and he did his best not to look too excited. He grabbed his bag and then bent over to tie his shoes while his daughter made the small trip to the window to see who was honking. He watched her posture change from building a case to relaxing in the knowledge that she had figured something out. He had hoped she would have left already.

"Oh boy," he said quietly.

"Well, well, well . . . I should have known it would be *her*," Jennifer said.

"We're just friends, and she's the closest to me. I would have asked you, but I knew the third degree I would get," he explained. He finished up with his shoes and was now on the move to pick up his smart tablet and keys.

"Yes, well, I've heard of girlfriends joining a club, but she's your constant companion on these trips, isn't she?"

"She has been doing it for years, long before I started—"

"And you and her are always on the same flights, going to the same destinations, and just seem to spend all the time together in these disaster zones. If it wasn't for the level of danger, I'd be a whole lot happier for you. Do you stay in this job for her?"

Cobb made sure not to answer too quickly for fear of implying that she was partially correct. He counted to ten, which allowed him the time to move to open the door and wave his daughter out.

"Well?"

Cobb focused on his keys and gave it a few seconds, then teased her a bit.

"Maybe yes, maybe no."

"I knew it!"

With the door locked and the note for the cleaner and lawn-care people secured in the mailbox, he decided to elaborate.

"Marie and I are friends, all right. If anything transpires, I'll let you know," he said. He thought his presentation was casual enough to be believable. He waved to her and then turned to kiss and hug his daughter good-bye.

"Of course," his daughter said. The tone was sarcastic, and she made no effort to hide her disbelief. She did make sure to wave to his ride and hug and kiss him good-bye. She held on to him longer than expected but then did let him go. He headed to his waiting transport as his daughter watched him. He could still feel her gaze on him.

"Don't make me regret this," she called out.

"You got it," he said without turning back.

As he closed in on the car, he felt more energized and excited by the new adventure he was off to. Many would call it a crisis or dangerous mission, but for him, it was yet another opportunity to "live a more interesting life."

ABOUT THE AUTHOR

In addition to creating the Birds of Flight series and the award-winning science-fiction stories *Future Prometheus* and *Intelligent Design*, Erickson holds a BA in psychology and sociology from Boston College and a master's degree in psychiatric social work from the Simmons School of Social Work. Certified in cognitive-behavioral treatment and a posttrauma specialist, he is also a senior instructor of psychology and counseling at Cambridge College and a senior therapist in a clinical group practice in Merrimack Valley, Massachusetts.

If you enjoyed this novel, please feel free to let others know about it. I would also appreciate it if you could leave a review on Amazon, Barnes & Noble, or wherever you purchased the novella. For more information on my other stories, please feel free to visit my websites and blog:

www.jmericksonindiewriter.com
www.jmericksonindiewriter.net
www.jmeindieblog.com

www.ingramcontent.com/pod-product-compliance
Lightning Source LLC
Chambersburg PA
CBHW020644130626
46552CB00003B/1397